THE YEAR
OF THE PANDA

Miriam Schlein
THE YEAR OF THE PANDA

Illustrated by Kam Mak

INSTRUCTIONAL RESOURCE CENTER
Evergreen School District 114
2205 N.E. 138 Avenue
Vancouver, WA 98684-7228

HarperTrophy
A Division of HarperCollinsPublishers

For information address HarperCollins Children's Books,
a division of HarperCollins Publishers, 10 East 53rd Street,
New York, NY 10022.
Typography by Andrew Rhodes

Library of Congress Cataloging-in-Publication Data
Schlein, Miriam.
    The year of the panda / by Miriam Schlein ; illustrated by
Kam Mak.
        p. cm.
    Summary: A Chinese boy rescues a starving baby panda, and,
in the process, learns why pandas are endangered, and what the
government is doing to save them.
    ISBN 0-690-04864-5.—ISBN 0-690-04866-1 (lib. bdg.)
    ISBN 0-06-440366-1 (pbk.)
    [1. Pandas—Fiction.   2. Wildlife rescue—Fiction.   3. Rare
animals—Fiction.   4. China—Fiction.]   I. Mak, Kam, ill.
II. Title.
PZ7.S347Ye   1990   89-71307
[Fic]—dc20   CIP
                                                                AC

First Harper Trophy edition, 1992.

THE YEAR
OF THE PANDA

1

Lu Yi opened his eyes.

Something was wrong.

He knew it right away.

Usually, it was quiet here on the farm. The voices of his mother and father—of course he knew these. Mr. Po, or Ho Yen, or Mrs. Chen, who lived on farms close by, he knew their voices, too. So well, they were like part of him.

But this was different. These were the voices of strangers, talking very loud with his father.

He leaned on one elbow and listened.

Usually, Lu Yi hated to get up in the morning. Most days his mother had to call him two or three times.

But today he jumped up and looked out. There were two men he had never seen before. Strangers were rare here, where he lived, in the shadow of the great, snow-covered mountains.

Who were they? And what did they want?

Lu Yi sat in the corner of the court-yard and listened.

He heard: "The government will not force you. They are *asking* you to move. For the reasons I have explained."

"It is your right to say no," the other man added.

Lu Yi's father looked at his mother. "Then we say no."

His mother nodded. Then the two strangers walked off.

"Are we moving, Father?"

Lu Yi looked around. The field of wheat. The vegetable garden. The beehives for honey. He was born here. He could not imagine living someplace else.

"Don't worry, son. I told the man no."

"How could we move?" said Lu Yi. "This land is our family's. It is yours now. Before that, it was your father's."

". . . and after my time," said his father, "it will be *your* land. Time now to work. And for you, school."

His father did not sound worried. Still, later on, he saw his father talking excitedly to Mr. Po.

Lu Yi knew that sometimes his father tried hard not to seem troubled when, in fact, he *was*. Lu Yi had the feeling this was one of those times. He also knew it was no use asking any more questions right now.

2

Busy weeks followed. Lu Yi helped cut and stack the ripe yellow wheat. The grain had to be threshed, dried, bagged. Then, what they did not use themselves they took to town, where it would be either sold or put on canal barges and taken to larger cities. When he was needed, Lu Yi did not go to school, but worked alongside his parents.

This was such a time. Lu Yi almost forgot about the two strangers and the talk about moving.

Then, one morning, he was awakened by angry shouts.

"Get away, you rascal . . . get out of there!"

Lu Yi jumped up from his sleeping mat and ran to the door. There was Mr. Po, wrestling with a large black-and-white animal next to his beehives. The animal had one paw stuck in a hive. Mr. Po was tugging at it.

Lu Yi stared. It was a daxiong mao (dah-shung mah-oo)—the great bear-cat. He had never seen one before. Daxiong mao lived high in the mountains. They never came down here.

At that moment, Mr. Po and the daxiong mao ended their wrestling match. For the bees burst out in an angry humming swarm. The two wrestlers parted abruptly. Mr. Po ran

toward his house. The daxiong mao dropped to all fours and clumsily ran up the mountain slope.

Mr. Po was furious. He ran to his house and came out with an old shotgun. Lu Yi's father stopped him.

"Are you crazy? You kill a daxiong mao and they will make us all move!"

Mr. Po seemed to calm down. Lu Yi's father let go of his arm. "Besides," he added, "you don't really want to shoot it. There are so few left, up there." He motioned toward the mist-covered mountains.

"Well . . . as long as they stay up there . . . and keep out of my hives."

Grumbling to himself, Mr. Po took the gun back to his house.

The daxiong mao—or giant panda, as some call it—is a very special animal. Living high in the mountains, it is a creature of mystery. It lives hidden, deep in the bamboo forests. Why did this one suddenly appear?

Now that the harvest was over, Lu Yi went back to school. As usual, he met his friend Ho Yen, and they walked together along the footpath to the schoolteacher's house. But who could think about school?

"Did you see it?"

"Of course I did."

As the boys walked and talked, they kept glancing up at the mountains, hoping they might get another glimpse of the daxiong mao.

"Maybe it'll come back."

"I hope not."

"Don't you want to see it?"

"Sure. But Mr. Po might shoot it!"

Lu Yi waved at Mrs. Chen as they walked by. She was working in her rice field.

"Why do you think it came down from the mountain?"

Ho Yen shrugged. "Why? I guess to get Mr. Po's honey. I don't blame it. Do you?"

Lu Yi walked silently for a while. Ho Yen made a joke of everything. Should he tell him the worry he had been keeping inside?

"I think we might have to move," he blurted out.

"Move?" For once Ho Yen became serious. "Why?"

"I think it has to do with the daxiong mao."

"What? Because the daxiong mao came to steal Mr. Po's honey. . . ?" Ho Yen started to laugh.

Lu Yi frowned. It was not a joke. "Didn't you hear what my father said?"

"Yes. He said, 'If you kill the daxiong mao, we will all have to move.' "

"So?"

Ho Yen shook his head. "He was

all excited. . . . He didn't want Mr.
Po to shoot. You know how grown-
ups are. They just say things sometimes."

"Not my father."

The two boys walked in silence
for a while. "Hmm," said Ho Yen
finally. "I can't see what one thing
has to do with the other. . . ."

Well, Mr. Po mended his beehives.
He quit his grumbling. There was
no more talk about moving. And,
for a while, everything was much
the same as before.

3

Then came the day Lu Yi always thought of, later on, as the day that changed his whole life. It started in an ordinary way. He and his father went to the upper slopes to gather firewood. As usual, his father carried the ax. Lu Yi carried a large sack for the wood. On the way back, his father would carry the wood-filled sack; Lu Yi would carry the ax.

As usual, woodpeckers clattered away on the tree trunks. Now and then a tiny furry vole scurried away from under their feet. Twice they surprised pheasants, which flew up from the leaves in a flurry.

They never had to chop down trees. There were enough fallen limbs on the ground, from big spruce trees, birches, and hemlocks. Lu Yi's father would chop these into pieces so that they could be carried more easily. Higher up the mountain were the bamboo forests. Usually rich and green, the bamboo now seemed dry and yellowish.

Lu Yi was looking at all these things when suddenly his father, off to the side in some underbrush, stretched out an arm. "Stay back, son."

He was peering down. Lu Yi followed his gaze. He saw a black-and-white mound.

A daxiong mao!

"Is it sleeping?"

His father shook his head. "I thought so at first. It's dead."

Lu Yi came closer. He stared. He had wanted to see a daxiong mao again. But not like this.

They turned away.

The sack was soon filled with wood. Lu Yi's father put it over his shoulder. Lu Yi took the ax. Then, as he paused to take a last look at the dead daxiong mao—wondering if it was the one that had wrestled with Mr. Po—Lu Yi heard a squeak. He turned. More squeaks. They seemed to come from a hollow tree. He peeked in.

"Father!"

His father, about twenty paces down the trail, laid down the sack and came back. Father and son peered into the tree hollow. His father reached in. He lifted something out. It was a small white creature, with darker fur on the shoulders and legs. It wiggled frantically.

Lu Yi gasped. It was about seven inches long. It was a baby daxiong mao.

"That was its mother . . . over there." Lu Yi's father pointed to the dead animal.

"Father, can we take it home?"

"If we don't, it will starve. Or wild dogs will get it." Lu Yi took that to mean yes.

He dropped the ax to the ground and reached out for the baby daxiong mao. Lu Yi's father tucked the ax into his belt and headed down the mountain. Lu Yi followed, the cub held close to his chest. Soon the little animal stopped squeaking and fell asleep.

4

Lu Yi's mother stared. "What are we going to do with it?" Then she put her hand out and touched the little animal in her son's arms. As soon as she did that, Lu Yi knew everything would be all right.

"I'll take care of it," he said. "I took care of the sick baby goat. Remember? I can do it. You know that, Mother."

It was true. He was good with the animals. Over Lu Yi's head, his mother and father nodded slightly.

"This doesn't mean you can forget about your other tasks."

"And your study."

"No, no. I'll do it all."

It was Lu Yi's task to help care for the animals. Every day he milked the two female goats, Nim and Lei. He made sure Bim and Bam, the two oxen, had feed. He checked to see if they had sores on their shoulders from the yoke. If so, he would rub in ointment. He threw corn to the chickens. And he cleaned out the courtyard, where the animals stayed at night. Lu Yi looked down. How hard could it be to take care of this little thing?

"Mother, could I have some milk?"

His mother gave him a small bowl of milk. Lu Yi sat with the little da-xiong mao in his lap. He tipped the bowl toward the animal's mouth. But the milk dribbled down its jaw.

"He's used to drinking from his mother."

The little daxiong mao lay back without moving.

"Maybe he's not hungry."

Meantime, in the courtyard, the other animals were restless. The chickens were squawking. Nim and Lei bleated a few times.

"You know, the other animals need your attention, too," Lu Yi's father said. "I'm taking some of this wood to old Mother Ting." He passed through the courtyard and walked off.

Lu Yi put the little daxiong mao down on a pile of hay and went about his other tasks. It was while he was milking Nim that he got his idea.

"Now, Nim . . ." He stroked the goat's neck. "You would not mind . . . would you?"

He picked up the baby daxiong mao and put its mouth on the goat's nipple. He gave a little squeeze. Some milk squirted into the baby's mouth.

"It has forgotten how to suck." Lu Yi's mother was standing there. He had not heard her come back out to the courtyard. "Squeeze again, son."

With a series of little squeezes, he fed the infant daxiong mao till it seemed to have enough. He laid it down in the corner, on some straw, and went about his other tasks. He finished later than usual. And he still had to do some school lessons.

He was yawning and writing when an excited Ho Yen stuck his head in the door. "I heard! Where is it?"

Lu Yi held his pad up. The little animal lay curled underneath, in his lap.

"Let me hold him." Without waiting for an answer, Ho Yen lifted the

little animal, which promptly began squealing and squirming. Ho Yen raised it high in the air. It squeaked louder. "I do that with my brother Wong's baby. She likes it."

"Put him down. This is not Wong's baby. You're scaring him."

Ho Yen squatted close to his friend and put the little animal on the ground. "Funny. It doesn't look like a daxiong mao. It looks more like a little pig." Ho Yen hopped up. "I have to go help my mother."

Lu Yi went back to his lessons. But somehow his mind was not on them. Where, he wondered, would the daxiong mao sleep? He finally placed it on a pile of hay in the corner of the courtyard. But just then his father came in with the oxen.

"This is not a good place," thought Lu Yi. "He'll be crushed by the other animals." So the first night the baby daxiong mao slept with Lu Yi, curled up close to his chest. The little animal liked the warmth of Lu Yi's body. It pushed up close to him. Lu Yi kept waking up. Hairs were tickling his chest. Then his mat became wet.

The next day, Lu Yi was sleepy as he went about his morning chores. His mother saw his mat out airing. She knew why, right away. "Maybe he can sleep in a basket," she said.

"He likes to be close to me."

"You're taking the place of his mother."

"Mmmm."

Lu Yi led Bim and Bam out. He held the two oxen as his father put on the yoke. Then he fed the little daxiong mao, again holding it up to the goat's nipple and squeezing gently.

Days, the baby daxiong mao seemed content to rest in the basket. When Lu Yi came home from school, he would take it out with him. His mother had fashioned a little sling out of an old pair of pants. When Lu Yi went to bring the goats in, the baby daxiong mao rode in the sling, peering out over Lu Yi's shoulder.

As week followed week, the baby daxiong mao thrived. Lu Yi noticed it was getting quite heavy to carry in the sling.

"There." He set the animal down. "I think I'm going to give you a name. I'll call you Su Lin."

Lu Yi's father was nearby. "I don't think it's a good idea to give it a name."

"Why, Father? All the other animals have names—except the chickens."

"We can't keep feeding a wild animal," said his father.

"We feed the others."

"The others work for us. We could not live without them. This is a wild animal. We can't keep it for long. For many reasons."

Lu Yi's father put a hand on his son's shoulder. "When you name a creature, you and it then have a connection. It will be harder for you, later on."

Lu Yi picked up the little animal and put it on his lap. "I'm connected to you already," he thought.

"What do you mean, later on?"

"Son, you didn't think you could keep . . . Su Lin forever. He will grow to be a strong and fierce animal."

"Where can he go?" Lu Yi could barely get the words out.

"I have spoken to the bargeman.

He has agreed to take him to Jinan. There is a zoo there. We can't wait long. He is getting too big."

"When?"

"I think you should start making the cage. Now."

5

Where Lu Yi lived, they had few
of the things that people in town had.
There was no electricity. No tele-
phones. Few roads. Most goods were
carried on barges on the canals. The
farmers would take their produce to
load onto the barges to take it to
town markets, where it could be
sold. But the barges carried more
than corn, honey, wheat, and vegetables. They carried news. Through
the bargemen, people in the country-
side would learn of what was happening in far-off places.

The news would travel in the other direction, too. Government officials in the cities would learn what was happening in isolated farm areas, such as where Lu Yi and his family lived.

There was another way that Lu Yi and his neighbors could get news. Sometimes, messengers were sent out from the cities with important news. Traveling on foot, along the footpaths, they would tack up notices along the way.

It was in this way that Lu Yi learned the answer to the question that had been on his mind: Why, suddenly, had that daxiong mao—Mr. Po's daxiong mao—come down from the mountains?

One morning the sound of hammering was heard. People stopped whatever they were doing. They knew what it meant and flocked to

the footpath. Sure enough, a man was hammering a notice on the tree.

Lu Yi ran out. Ho Yen, already there, beckoned him over. "It's all about the daxiong mao," his friend whispered. "Listen."

The messenger was speaking. "Up there"—he pointed to the mist-shrouded mountains—"lives the daxiong mao. All over the world, the daxiong mao is beloved. But this is the only place in the world it lives. And now it is in trouble. If we do not help it, there will soon be no more daxiong mao in the world."

News messengers were always long-winded—maybe because most of their days were spent walking alone along the footpaths. So they enjoyed talking when they had a chance. This one went on, and on, and on. Though the people were interested, they were also impatient.

"We know that," they interrupted. "Get to the point."

"Look up there, my friends," the man said, pointing.

All eyes looked up toward the mountains—almost expecting to see more daxiong mao appear out of the forests.

"Look carefully. Even from here, you can see what is happening. The bamboo forests are yellow and dry. The bamboo has died. The daxiong mao have nothing to eat up there. That is why they are coming down. They are starving."

Mrs. Chen's mother spoke up. "I have lived here many, many years. This never happened before. Why now?"

"Why now?" The man took a cloth from his pocket and wiped his forehead. Everyone waited nervously.

"That is so, Mother. It has not happened while you were here." It was clear the man wished to speak to the old woman with respect. "But it *did* happen," he added, "before you lived here. The bamboo up there dies every sixty years. Then it takes two or three years for new shoots to grow. The daxiong mao are having a famine. That is why they are coming down. They are desperate for food."

The Chinese people understand famine. The older ones, especially, murmured, remembering sad times.

Mr. Po spoke up in his raspy voice. "That may be. But I am a poor man. I cannot afford to feed daxiong mao with my honey." He began to describe at great length his battle with the daxiong mao, until the stranger stopped his flow of words.

"We do not expect you to. But

there is a plan to help the daxiong mao to live through this time. We are asking your help. We know you cannot afford to feed these animals. So the government will supply the food. In the coming weeks, helicopters will drop sweet potatoes and corn. Place this along the high ridge of your fields and grazing land. Starving daxiong mao will eat it. But don't approach them. They are starving, desperate animals. Remember, a daxiong mao can be fierce."

His audience, quiet for so long, all began to speak at once.

"I don't have time. . . ."

"There are hungry people! Why feed animals?"

"Where is this money coming from?"

"The money to save the daxiong mao comes from the government of the People's Republic of China. And even more money comes from the United States and other countries. They all care about the daxiong mao. The daxiong mao was once the gift of kings. Now there are just a few left. If we do not help them now, there will soon be no more in the world. And never will be, ever again. . . ."

"Mister, mister . . ." Ho Yen had gone up to the man. "The daxiong mao lived here long, long before people. Yes?"

"That's right."

"When the bamboo died before, we were not here. Who fed them then?"

"Not very long ago," said the man, "there were bamboo forests where your farms are now. When the mountain bamboo died, the daxiong mao came down here. Right here." He thumped the earth with his foot. "Here they would find different kinds of bamboo growing that had not died out. They could stay here till the upper forests were green once again. Now they cannot do that."

Ho Yen looked thoughtful. "Then this—right here, where we live—is the daxiong mao's land. . . ."

Mr. Po spoke up. "Nonsense! Animals cannot own land!"

"People have to eat, too." Mrs. Chen's mother's voice quavered. "I am an old woman. I cannot move. My son worked so hard to clear this land. . . ."

"Mother, no one will ever force you off your land here. But for those who wish to move elsewhere, the government will pay for it."

"I was right," thought Lu Yi. "The talk about moving *does* have to do with the daxiong mao."

"There is one thing I would like you to do," said the man. "Report every daxiong mao you see."

Everyone's head moved slightly. They all looked at Lu Yi. Yet nobody said anything. Not even Mr. Po. They were waiting for him to do it—to tell about Su Lin. He stood there, his heart pounding. He had, for days now, managed to find one excuse after another to put off constructing the cage. But now, the man would take Su Lin anyway. His mother squeezed his arm gently. Lu Yi opened his mouth. Nothing came out.

The man did not seem to notice any of this. "There is to be no shooting of a daxiong mao," he said. His eyes went to Mr. Po. "For some time it has been against the law to do that. It is now an even more serious offense."

Then he smiled. "But here is the good news. The government will give a reward of three hundred yuan to any person who helps save a da-xiong mao."

"Three hundred yuan!"

"Three hundred yuan!"

There was a hum of excited talk.

"Enough to buy a sewing machine!"

"Not enough for a bicycle."

"Maybe an old one . . ."

The only one to look glum was Mr. Po. "I should have wrestled the beast to the ground . . . tied him up. I could have done it."

Everyone smiled. Mr. Po was a puny fellow.

The messenger nodded. "It's a good reward. It shows how serious the government is about this matter." He picked up his hammer, his roll of notices, his screwed-up paperful of tacks, and got ready to move on. He did not seem to notice how the villagers had suddenly gotten quiet again, and were now smiling and staring at Lu Yi.

Why did no one say anything—not even Ho Yen—although Ho Yen looked as though he were about to burst with excitement? The truth was they did not have much trust in matters to do with the government. It was up to Lu Yi himself to tell the man. And he couldn't do it.

His father finally spoke up. "We have a daxiong mao."

"You have a daxiong mao?" The messenger was astonished. "What do you mean, you *have* one?"

The crowd surrounded Lu Yi. They all walked toward his house. Ho Yen threw an arm around his friend's shoulder. "Three hundred yuan. What are we going to buy?"

Lu Yi shook his head. He wasn't even thinking about the reward. All he could think about was Su Lin, and the day they found him. How he had carried him down the mountainside. How tiny he was, and how helpless. Now he was bigger. More furry. The black band on his back was darker. His little pompon ears stood erect. And he could walk very well.

Up ahead, Lu Yi's mother and father were explaining to the messenger how everything happened. When they all entered the courtyard, Lu Yi stopped short. Su Lin's basket was there. But it was tipped over. And it was empty.

He ran over and looked behind it. He began whistling. Sometimes Su Lin would squeak in answer to his whistle. But now, nothing.

The gate to the courtyard was open.

"He could have gone outside."

"Where would he go?"

"He has never done that before."

"There is always a first time."

"He is not here." Lu Yi's father had been looking in the shed where he kept seed, burlap bags, tools.

"We'll have to search the area."

Lu Yi was on his way out when his mother called out, "Don't worry. Come in here. Look."

The little daxiong mao lay against the wall, snuggled against Lu Yi's sleeping mat, entangled and half covered with Lu Yi's jacket. He was snoring peacefully, making little squeaking sounds, his chest moving rhythmically.

"Oh." Lu Yi sank to his knees.

"Those things have your body smell on them," said his mother. "They make him feel safe."

What a mixed-up way to feel.

Happy to find Su Lin. Unhappy that he was about to lose Su Lin.

The little daxiong mao opened his eyes. Lu Yi picked him up.

"He was all but dead when we found him," said Lu Yi's father.

Lu Yi's mother described how her son had been able to get Nim, the goat, to give the baby daxiong mao his milk.

The man reached out for the little daxiong mao. "You've done a good job . . . ouch!" He looked at his hand, scratched by Su Lin's claw.

"Tell me. What were you going to do with him?"

"Send him to the zoo," said Lu Yi.

Lu Yi's father broke in. "When does my son get his reward?" This, too, was an important subject that no one else seemed to be thinking about.

"When the animal and my report are delivered."

Lu Yi knew it was no disgrace to cry. Still, he turned away. Su Lin would be leaving today. Right now. At least he himself understood what was happening. Su Lin would not.

"What will happen to him?" he managed to ask.

"In the Wolong Reserve there is a Rescue Center for daxiong mao. They are cared for very well there."

"Wolong." Wolong was far. He would never again see Su Lin.

"This little fellow will be the youngest one there. You have named him?"

"Su Lin," whispered Lu Yi.

"I will tell them. At least that will be one thing familiar for this little one."

"I will get you a basket so you can carry him," said Lu Yi's mother.

"Oh, no. I can't take him with me today. I have a hundred kilometers to travel yet. I couldn't care for him properly. We will have to make different arrangements." He looked at Lu Yi. "You won't mind taking care of this fellow for a short time more?"

Lu Yi grinned.

Then the man explained exactly how Su Lin would be taken to the Daxiong Mao Rescue Center.

As he listened, Lu Yi grinned even more.

6

Lu Yi, his parents, and Ho Yen stood at the edge of the north field. Their eyes searched the skies.

This was the plan the messenger had made with them last week: Su Lin would be picked up and taken by helicopter to the Daxiong Mao Rescue Center accompanied by Lu Yi, who would stay at the center for a short while, till another helicopter could take him back.

They scanned the sky in every direction.

"This is the right day," said Lu Yi anxiously.

"It is still very early," said his mother.

Lu Yi held Su Lin in his arms. In a small sack that now lay on the ground he had some supplies: a bottle of goat milk and some mashed-up yams.

"Listen." Ho Yen put his hand to his ear. It was a far-off hum. Bit by bit it got louder. It was definitely the helicopter.

In the village, tools, pots, sewing were all put down. Animals were tethered. Everyone stopped what he or she was doing. The copter finally appeared from behind a cloud.

The neighbors gathered in a little group around Lu Yi. All faced upward, looking at the copter.

"How small it is."

"What keeps it up, I wonder. . . ."

"I don't understand any modern things."

"Not all of them are so good."

"Some are."

"It's not coming down," someone shouted.

"It's not even dropping anything!"

"All talk, no action, how can you trust the government anyhow?" Mr. Po walked away from the group.

The copter flew eastward till it was out of sight. But in little more than half an hour, it reappeared. It hovered about two hundred yards away from them. Then it began to come down. They ran to the spot.

"Don't stand under it," yelled Ho Yen.

The copter descended, then gently hit the ground.

The pilot stuck his head out. "Don't come too close!" He tossed out two large sacks of yams and a sack of corn. "Spread the food up there, on the ridge. Not all in one place."

He took his goggles off and smiled. "Where are my passengers?"

"Here's your jacket, son." Lu Yi's mother hugged him. She patted Su Lin. "Good bye, little visitor."

Lu Yi handed up Su Lin, then his small sack of supplies, his jacket, and his basket.

"Lucky devil," Ho Yen said. "Remember everything, so you can tell me about it."

Lu Yi waved. Abruptly, the copter lifted straight into the air.

The pilot did some things with levers and switches for a moment. Then he turned to Lu Yi. "My name's Hu Shang. And you?"

"I'm Lu Yi. And this . . ." He put his head down on the little daxiong mao's furry back. "This is Su Lin." He added, "We thought you

had forgotten about us, when you flew right by."

"Oh, no. I had a food drop to make farther on."

They flew westward, the sun behind them. To the left were mountain peaks. To the right were small farms, dividing the earth into brown and green and yellow squares. Lu Yi could see people below, doing all their everyday things. It all looked comfortable and familiar.

Lu Yi told Hu Shang about how he had found the orphaned daxiong mao and its dead mother. Hu Shang told Lu Yi how it was to grow up in a large city.

"How did you learn to fly?" asked Lu Yi.

"In the army," said Hu Shang.

The slight humming of the motor had lulled the baby daxiong mao to sleep. It was not until Lu Yi took out some food that the cub, smelling it, woke up. Lu Yi gave him some goat milk from a jug, spilling about half of it. "It's easier," he said, "getting it right from the goat." He then gave Su Lin some mashed yam from his fingers. The cub licked it off, gave a small burp, then put his head down and slept.

"Oh," Lu Yi sighed.

Hu Shang turned to him. "Airsick?"

Lu Yi shook his head. "No." He stroked the small black-and-white furball on his lap. "Just thinking. What will he think, when I leave him alone?"

"He won't be alone."

"What I mean is, I'll miss him."

"You know you could not have kept him for long."

Lu Yi nodded. Of course he knew that. But what you know in your brain and what you feel in your heart can be two very different things.

"Here we are," said Hu Shang after a while. He, too, had been quiet, occupied with his own thoughts. He pointed.

Lu Yi peered down. He saw a group of small buildings, surrounded by forest. For a moment the copter hung suspended in the sky. Then, almost magically, they drifted downward. They landed, bouncing down gently onto a small clearing. A man wearing a turban ran out to greet them.

"Welcome." He smiled at Lu Yi, then looked at Su Lin. "Well . . . I guess this is our new guest." He turned to Hu Shang. "You, my friend, have another flight."

"Today?"

"Yes."

They walked toward a small brick building. The turbaned man, whose name was Zilin, had flung his arm about Hu Shang's shoulder and began talking nonstop. "In Zang-Fu," he explained, "three farmers carried down a daxiong mao from the upper slopes. It seemed to them quite ill. It would not eat anything they offered. They have it now in a hut. We have to go get it right now. I'm to go with you."

By now they had reached the small building. Lu Yi followed the two men in. Inside was a woman not like any woman Lu Yi had ever seen. She was tall—taller than his father. She had long yellow hair, and a long thin nose.

Her face lit up when she saw Su Lin. She started to reach for him, then stopped. "Please put him down on this table," she said. She spoke slowly in putongua, the common language, which is spoken all through China.

Su Lin, on this strange cold surface, tried to get up. His feet slipped. He started to squeak in alarm. His squeaking stopped when the woman gently pushed open his jaws and peered into his mouth with a small flashlight. As she examined him, she talked to herself, this time in English. "He has teeth," she murmured. "Oh yes, you do have teeth," she said, pulling her hand away quickly and addressing Su Lin directly.

Lu Yi did not know what she was saying. He began to feel anxious. Was there something wrong with Su Lin?

Taking a tape measure, the woman measured Su Lin's back and legs; then she looked at his claws. She kept writing things down in a notebook. Finally she turned to Lu Yi and spoke again in putongua. "How big was he when you found him?"

"Oh. Very small." Lu Yi showed

her the size with his hands. "But he has grown, oh, ten or eleven centimeters, at least. And he is much, much heavier than before. Maybe three kilo . . ."

The yellow-haired woman put up her hand. "Wait, wait. Please, not so fast."

Lu Yi repeated what he had said, only more slowly. Then he went on. "And he can walk and run now. When I found him, he could not even stand on his feet. The markings on his shoulders were very, very pale. . . ."

Lu Yi, in his enthusiasm, again began to talk faster, using some words in Sechuan dialect, which is what he spoke at home all the time. It was only at school that he spoke putongua.

"Whoa," said Hu Shang. In English, he explained to the woman what Lu Yi had said.

She nodded.

Lu Yi spoke up. "He was so little, and so scared and alone, and crying, when we found him. I'm sorry, I did not think to measure him. . . ."

The woman nodded. "Oh, my. You should not apologize," she said. "Whatever you did, you did absolutely right." She flashed a smile. "He would not have been in better health if he had two vets caring for him."

Lu Yi smiled doubtfully. He could not understand everything that she said. But she seemed pleased. He could see that.

"It's a little late to do this," said Hu Shang, "but I should introduce you two. Dr. Di, this is Lu Yi. Lu Yi, this is Dr. Diana Fleming. She is here from the States. She is a daxiong mao expert."

The two shook hands.

Dr. Di turned to Hu Shang. "I

hate to do this to you, but there is a rescued daxiong mao out past the town of Zang-Fu. It would be good if you could get him out here to-night."

The pilot nodded. "Zilin told me. They're checking the copter over. I'll have something to eat, and we'll be off."

Lu Yi, during this discussion, had moved close to the table and put an arm about Su Lin. But he did not pick him up. He was, he supposed, no longer in charge of the little da-xiong mao.

"I'll be back tomorrow and take you home," said Hu Shang, patting Lu Yi's shoulder. "You can sleep in my room tonight." Then he hurried out.

"Would you like to see where Su Lin will stay?" asked the yellow-haired woman.

"Yes, ma'am."

"Everyone here calls me Dr. Di."

"Yes, ma'am, Dr. Di."

Dr. Di put her notebook and flashlight up on a shelf. Lu Yi picked up Su Lin and followed Dr. Di out the door.

They walked just a few steps and came to a row of cages. Dr. Di took out a key and opened one of them.

Lu Yi stared. What a terrible place. A floor of cement. Thick bars along the front. In the corner a big pile of branches. And wire in front of the bars.

He clutched Su Lin tighter.

"I know," said Dr. Di. "You are thinking that this is a terrible place. But Su Lin will only be in here for a few days. At first, we must watch the newcomers quite closely. This is the best place to do it. Come. Put him in."

Lu Yi set Su Lin down on the hard

cement. Dr. Di shut the door. The little animal stood and gazed through the wire. Dr. Di took Lu Yi by the shoulders and gently turned him around. "He'll be all right," she said. "Let me show you what we do here."

They walked past a long wooden building. "That's where we sleep. And that . . ." Dr. Di pointed to another building from which smoke rose. "That's the cookhouse."

Now they came to a planted area, with five or six different kinds of things growing. Lu Yi paused. "It's all bamboo." He squatted down, held a leaf. "I've never seen these kinds. Look at this!" One type had a sort of twisted stem. He looked up at Dr. Di questioningly.

"We are trying out different kinds of bamboo," she said, "to see if it will grow here. The twisted one is from Nepal. That"—she pointed to a plot of bamboo with purple stalks—"is from Japan. This one over here is from Florida." She pointed to some pale-green bamboo with a slim-as-a-pencil stalk. "If it grows well here, we will plant it on the lower slopes. Then, when the local fountain, arrow, and umbrella bamboo die again, the daxiong mao will still have these other types to eat."

"You mean it will be an emergency food supply," said Lu Yi.

"Exactly!"

They walked a bit farther and came to two young men who were constructing large wood-barred boxes.

"These are carrying cages. Rescue teams of four men each go up in the forests. They bring back starving daxiong mao in these. Six have been brought in this way. . . ."

"Believe me," said one of the men, "they are not easy to carry."

"I can imagine," agreed Dr. Di.

She and Lu Yi walked on. "We have seventeen daxiong mao here."

"Where are they?"

"Right here."

They had come to a high wire fence. Behind it was untouched land. It sloped sharply upward. There were rocks, ledges, some tall trees. High in one tree, a daxiong mao was sitting on a branch, looking down at them. The wild area, Lu Yi saw, was divided into separate large spaces, divided by wire fences. Close to a rock, he saw, was a large daxiong mao sleeping flat out, on its back, snoring gently.

"That's Ling-Ling," said Dr. Di. "He was carried down in one of those boxes. The one in the tree is Chi-Chi. A farmer had shot her. Someone from his village told a bargeman. That's how we learned about her.

We sent out a team. They found her, not far off, fortunately not too seriously wounded."

Lu Yi thought of Mr. Po back home. "What happened to the man who shot her?"

"He was fined fifty yuan."

Lu Yi made a mental note to tell this to Mr. Po when he got back home.

"So. This is the kind of place where Su Lin will live very soon," said Dr. Di.

"His whole life?" asked Lu Yi.

"No. For about a year and a half. Then we will do one of two things. We may take him to another part of China, where the bamboo forests have not died. Or, when the bamboo has regrown here on this mountain, we can free him right here."

"But when the bamboo dies again . . ." Lu Yi began.

Dr. Di interrupted. "The lifetime of a daxiong mao is about thirty years. The bamboo up here dies only every sixty years or so. So it will not happen again during Su Lin's lifetime."

"But the daxiong mao living then?" said Lu Yi.

"The same thing will happen. They will have to be rescued or most of them will starve to death. Unless"—Dr. Di hesitated; Lu Yi waited—"unless a different kind of bamboo can be planted on the lower slopes."

Lu Yi knew why she had hesitated. "Where there are farms now," he added. "Where I live."

"That's right."

"That's why they want us to move."

"No one knew about the daxiong mao problem back then, when your family settled there," answered Dr. Di.

A loud gong rang out.

"Dinnertime," said Dr. Di. They headed for the cookhouse. On the way they passed Su Lin's cage. The little daxiong mao was no longer standing at the bars, looking forlorn. Instead, he was stretched out on the pile of branches, fast asleep.

Several men were sitting at a long table in the cookhouse. Dr. Di introduced Lu Yi. They nodded and smiled. "You've brought us a baby daxiong mao?" said one named Wo Ping.

"A healthy one?" asked another.

Dr. Di beamed. "He took wonderful care of the animal."

Cook brought in bowls of vegetables, pork, and rice. Suddenly Lu Yi realized how hungry he was.

*　*　*

That night Lu Yi slept on a mat in Hu Shang's room. He was awakened after a while by a humming sound. He leaned on one elbow and listened. It was the copter. It must be Hu Shang.

Lu Yi pushed his feet into his sandals and went out.

In the dark night sky what looked like a red star approached. It hovered, then descended.

Dr. Di now appeared, a spot of white light from her flashlight bouncing on the ground in front of her.

Zilin hopped out of the copter, then turned to reach for a stretcher.

"Grab an end. Hold tight." Together, they all eased the stretcher out. On it was a large, very limp daxiong mao. The animal's head lolled back at a funny angle. Was it dead?

"I gave him a second shot ten minutes ago," said Zilin. "We've got to work fast."

"If he awakens too soon . . ." Hu Shang shook his head.

Dr. Di flashed her light on the animal. "Let's take him right to the cage. I'll examine him there."

They carried the unconscious animal to a cage. They set the stretcher down. There, kneeling in the dark, with the help of her flashlight, Dr. Di examined the newcomer. She shone her light into his ears, eyes, nose, and mouth. She examined his paws. She put a round metal disc on the animal's chest, and with her stethoscope listened to his heartbeat. Winding a cloth around the animal's leg, she then squeezed a little rubber bulb seven or eight times. Then she listened. She scribbled some numbers in her notebook. Next, she jabbed fast with a needle. Blood slowly filled a small glass tube. Dr. Di put a rubber stopper on the top, then stood up. They all left the cage; Hu Shang locked the door.

"It's a male," said Dr. Di. "About eight years old. Heartbeat weak. Blood pressure low. Infection in right ear. Large lump on his head."

Lu Yi listened. "How can you tell how old he is?"

"By the condition of his teeth," said Dr. Di. "How worn down they are."

From a spigot, she filled a bowl with water and handed it to Lu Yi. "Put this in his cage. You can slip it in under the bars."

Lu Yi went back and slid the bowl of water under the bars. The daxiong mao was now shaking his head, grunting. His paws twitched. His eyes opened. He stared groggily at

Lu Yi. Then the animal's head dropped back. He began to snore.

Lu Yi walked over to the cage where his own Su Lin was. He was sleeping peacefully.

Lu Yi was very quiet when he went back to Hu Shang's room. He slid noiselessly onto his sleeping mat. Hu Shang was already asleep. How tired he must be. Before long, except for the hooting of an owl in the distance, there was not a sound to be heard at the Daxiong Mao Rescue Center.

7

Quite early, the breakfast gong sounded. Lu Yi sighed. Morning seemed to come so fast. Hu Shang, he saw, was already gone.

Lu Yi made his way to the cook-house and slid onto the end of a bench. Cook brought him some tea, some wheat cereal, and fried bread.

Everyone was listening to Hu Shang. Zilin occasionally dropped in a remark. It seemed when they had reached the small cluster of farms at the foot of Ming-Dang Peak it was already dark. Landing the copter, they had frightened a flock of goats. Their bleating and baaing was something to hear.

"They then lost their fear, came close, and began to nibble on the copter," Zilin said. He picked up the story from there, letting Hu Shang concentrate on his breakfast.

". . . Three grandfathers were on guard outside a hut. They told us that as they were dragging the da-xiong mao to the hut, he suddenly reared up and roared. In desperation, they knocked the animal out with a rock. Then they put him in the hut. . . ."

The pilot picked up the tale. "We opened the door very slowly. We thought at first the poor thing was dead."

"How did you get him to the copter?"

"We dropped a net around him. We put him in a cart. By that time, everybody was out helping. Together, we lifted him into the copter."

"They were not sad," said Zilin, "to wave goodbye to their guest."

"You know," Hu Shang added, "they did not even know they would get a reward. Yet they did everything they could to save the animal."

"Why . . . ?"

"One of the elders said to me: 'Daxiong mao is rare and mysterious, like a god, living in the mist of the mountains.'"

"Mr. Po certainly did not share this feeling," thought Lu Yi, smiling.

One of the men at the table said something in his own dialect.

"He says," said Hu Shang, "What's so funny?"

Lu Yi told them about Mr. Po, and how his wrestling match with the daxiong mao was ended by the bees.

They soon all got up to go about their jobs.

"We'll leave in about two hours," said Hu Shang. "You can find something to do here in the meantime?"

"Oh, yes."

"Come help me," said Wo Ping. Lu Yi went with Wo Ping to prepare food for the animals. As they chopped up apples and carrots and filled baskets with corn and yams, Wo Ping told Lu Yi how he happened to be working here.

"I am a student of animal husbandry at the university at Shandong. This is part of my studies."

Lu Yi thought this strange. To him, study meant learning reading and writing, and maybe some history and geography. How interesting it would be to study animals.

When the food was ready, they

took it around. They came to Su Lin's cage. Wo Ping pulled out a key and opened it. "You can go in and give her her food."

Seeing Lu Yi, Su Lin began to make little squeaking sounds. Lu Yi took Su Lin in his arms. Then he turned, puzzled.

"Her?"

Wo Ping shrugged. "We don't know right now whether it's a him or a her. It's very hard to tell with daxiong mao. It's just about impossible when they're young."

Lu Yi had never thought about that. Hugging Su Lin, he did not care whether it was a she or a he.

Hu Shang approached. "I thought I'd find you here. We're about ready to leave."

Lu Yi put the little daxiong mao down. He left the cage quickly. He would never see Su Lin again. He

walked away quickly, thinking it would be easiest if he did not look back. But he did look back—once. Su Lin had his—or her—nose in the food they had brought in. Lu Yi walked away, not turning around again.

Dr. Di was outside her office. "I want to thank you." As usual, she spoke slowly, in putongua. "And I want to ask you something."

"Yes?"

"Would you like to come and work here for a time? You can be a student aide, like Wo Ping."

Lu Yi was speechless. Would he like it! Of course he would like it. But how could he leave his mother and father? They needed his help.

Dr. Di put a hand on his shoulder. "I know it is really your parents who must make this decision. I have written a letter to them." She handed him an envelope. Lu Yi's face flushed. His parents did not read very well. Would they understand it?

As though reading his mind, Dr. Di went on. "I am sure they will have questions. They can talk it over with our road messenger when he comes through again. You have a good understanding of animals, Lu Yi. The time here could help you decide whether you want to study to become a scientist who works with animals."

A scientist! Lu Yi had always thought he would be a farmer, like his father, and *his* father before him.

"My father needs my help, in the fields and with the animals." Lu Yi frowned. "How could I just go away?"

Dr. Di gave him a quick hug. "You must talk it over with your mother and father."

The helicopter engine was on, the propeller spinning above them. Hu Shang beckoned. Lu Yi climbed in the door.

"Take good care of Su Lin," he shouted.

The copter rose straight up. Then they flew along in the mountain's shadow, toward home.

Afterward

The reader can guess a lot of what happens later on. Wanting the best for their son, Lu Yi's parents let him go work at the Panda Rescue Center as a first step to his becoming an animal-research scientist.

With Lu Yi's three-hundred-yuan reward money they are able to pay for a helper on their farm to take Lu Yi's place. Sometimes, when he can, Lu Yi comes home to help out.

And, further in the future, when Lu Yi's parents are older, they, like many of their neighbors, do give up their farm and, with government financial assistance, move to a town, thus allowing their farmland to become wild once again, so that in times of future bamboo die-offs, pandas will be able to come down from the upper mountains to find bamboo on the lower slopes.

The basic details in the book are based on fact. The reward for panda rescue (and the penalty for harming one), the food drops, the rescue teams, the encouragement of peasants to relocate from the lower slopes, are all part of the Chinese government's strong efforts to save the panda—an animal they proudly consider part of their national heritage.

A number of American scientists—like "Dr. Di"—have been working in cooperation with Chinese scientists to help save the panda.